WHY FROG AND SNAKE CAN'T BE FRIENDS

Mama Frog had a son, and Mama Snake also had a son. One morning both children went out to play. Mama Snake called after her child, "Watch out for things with sharp claws and teeth that gnaw. Don't lose your way in the jungle, baby, and be back to the burrow before dark."

"Clawsangnaws," sang Snake, as he went looping through the grass. "Beware of the Clawsangnaws!"

Mama Frog called after her son, "Watch out for things that nip or bite. Don't go into the jungle alone, dear. Don't fight, and get home before night."

F R O G

"Niporbite," sang Frog, as he went hopping from stone to stone. "Beware of the Niporbite!"

3

Snake was singing his Clawsangnaws song, and Frog was singing of Niporbites, when they met along the way. They had never met before.

"Who are you?" asked Frog. "Are you a Niporbite?" And he prepared to spring out of reach.

"Oh, no! I'm Snake, called by my Mama 'Snakeson'. I'm slick, lithe, and slithery. Who are you? Are you a Clawsangnaws?" And he got ready to move, just in case.

4

"No, no! I'm Frog, called by my Mama 'Frogchild'. I'm hip, quick, and happy."

They stood and stared at each other, then they said together, "You don't look anything like me."

5

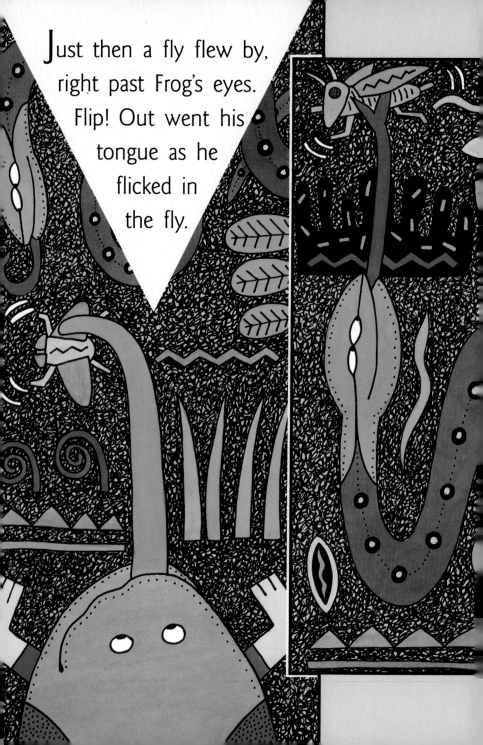

Just then a fly flew by, right past Frog's eyes. Flip! Out went his tongue as he flicked in the fly.

A bug whizzed past Snake's nose. Flash! Snake flicked out his tongue and caught the bug. They looked in admiration at each other and smiled. They felt at ease with each other, like old friends.

"Let's play," said Frog. "Since you're not a Niporbite, and I'm not a Clawsangnaws, we could play together."

7

Frog and Snake started playing games. "Watch this," said Frog. He crouched down and counted, "One a fly, two a fly, three a fly, four!" He popped way up into the air, somersaulted, and came down — whop! "Can you do that, Snake? It's called the Frog-Hop."

8

Snake slid to a nearby mound to try it. He got to the top of the slope, stood on the tip of his tail and tossed himself into the air. Down he came — flop! — in a tangle of coils. He laughed and tried again.

Then Snake said, "Watch this!" He stretched out at the top of the mound and counted, "One a bug, two a bug, three a bug, four!" Then swoosh! He slithered down the slope on his stomach.

"Try that, Frog. It's called the Snake- Slither."

Frog lay on his stomach and slipped
down the hill. His arms and legs
flailed about as he slithered.
He turned over at the
bottom of the slope,
—blump! — and
rolled up in
a lump.

All afternoon the two friends slithered and slid and flopped and hopped. Sometimes Snake was best, and sometimes Frog was best. One game led to another and the day sped by. As the sun began to set, the two friends remembered their promise to be home before dark.

"Good-bye," said Snake. "It's been fun." And he gave Frog a big hug. He squeezed him tightly — it felt good to have a friend like Frog. In fact, it felt so good that he squeezed him even more tightly.

"Ow! Easy!" croaked Frog. "Not too tight!"

"Sorry," said Snake, loosening his hug hold. "My, but you feel good, good enough to eat."

Frog laughed. "I like you," he said. "You're my very best friend."

Then off they went, frog-hopping and snake-slithering, all the way home.

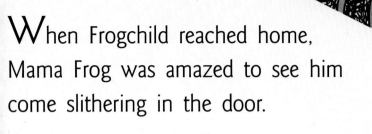

When Frogchild reached home, Mama Frog was amazed to see him come slithering in the door.

"Now, what is this, eh?" she said. "Look at you, all covered with grass and dirt. I can tell you haven't been playing in ponds or bogs with the good frogs. Where have you been all day, and what's happened to your legs?"

"Nothing, Mama," said Frogchild. "It's just my Snake-Slither."

At the mention of snake, Mama Frog paled. "Snake? What snake?" she croaked.

"Snake-Slither," said Frogchild. "My best friend, Snakeson, taught it to me today."

"Snakeson," gasped Mama Frog. "Did you say SNAKEson?"

Mama Frog trembled and turned a pale green. "Listen, Frogchild, listen carefully to what I have to say." She pulled her son close. "Snakes eat the likes of you and me. They crush you in their coils, they hide poison in their tongues. Snakeson comes from a bad family. You keep away from him, you hear? You be sure to hop out of Snakeson's reach if ever you meet again. And stop this slithering foolishness. Slithering's not for frogs."

Frogchild gulped as he thought of the games he'd played with Snakeson. He remembered Snakeson's hug.

"Now. Sit down and eat your dinner, child," said Mama Frog. "And remember, I'm not fattening frogs for snakes, eh?"

Snake, too, reached home. "I'm hungry, Ma," he said, hopping into the house.

"Oh! What a sight you are!" said Mama Snake. "Now where have you been all day?"

"In the jungle, Mama, with my new friend. See what he taught me."

"You look ridiculous," hissed his mother, as Snakeson flipped into the air and flopped onto the ground in a tangled mess. "What new friend taught you that?"

"My frog friend, Frogchild," said Snake.

"Frog? Did you say Frog?" hissed Mama Snake, showing her fangs. "You mean you played all day with a frog and you come home hungry? Now listen, Snakeson, frogs are to eat, not to play with. Frogs are delicious people. Eating frogs is a custom in our family, Snakeson, and hopping isn't. So cut it out, you hear me?"

"But Mama, I can't eat Frogchild. He's a friend," wailed Snakeson.

"Friend or not," said Mama, "next time you meet him, play all you like, but when you get hungry his game is up. Catch him and eat him!"

21

The next morning Snake was up early. He remembered his mother's words, and the delicious feel of his frog friend when they hugged. He slithered over to Frog's house.

"Frogchild," he called, "come and play.

"My mother taught me a new game, and I'd love to teach it to you."

"I bet you would," called Frog, "but I'm not coming."

"You don't know what you're missing," hissed Snake.

"Yes, I do," laughed Frog, "and I know what you're missing, too."

"Aha!" said Snake. "I see your mother has been talking to you, too."

Snake sighed. There was nothing more to say or do, so he slithered quietly away.

Frog and
Snake never forgot
the day when they played
together as friends. Neither ever
again had that much fun with anybody.

Today you will see them, quiet and alone in
the sun, still as stone. They are deep in
thought, remembering that day of games in
the jungle. Both of them wonder, "What if
we had just kept on playing together, and
no one had ever said anything?"

But from that day to this, Frog and
Snake have never played
together again.